The Kingdo

impspired@gmail.com

Cover design by Bhavya Pal

Artwork by Pat Cosgrave

ISBN: 978-1-914130-93-9

The Kingdom Reviews

These heart-warming, atmospheric stories have a folklore quality that taps into an ancient Irish tradition of oral storytelling. A set of interlinked tales, they carry the charm and appeal of a bygone age, of an otherworldly place, and conjure up a universe that is both ancient and familiar to us in which the characters of *The Kingdom* wind their way in and out of each other's lives. The sequence contains stories of love and loss, of heartbreak and joy, stories that are told with a clarity of wisdom and a celebration of community that seems much needed in today's fractured age.

Bernie McGill, The Butterfly Cabinet, 2014, Sleepwalkers, 2014, The Watch House, 2017, This train is for…, 2022.

It's as if we have stepped through a veil into a world that is the same but slightly out-of-kilter. We know these valleys and the people who live there; we recognise their dreams, their strengths and failings, their achievements and disappointments, but we take heart because the 'fates in that place are kindly.'

This could be our world in a gentler time when people had 'a kind of knowing', an inherited knowledge and appreciation of folklore and history which modern worlds have lost.

Mary Farrell's The Kingdom is a must read filled with gifts unexpected, not just for those who dwell there, but those of us who leaf its pages.

Kate Murphy, storyteller and facilitator, a regular contributor to My Story on BBC Radio Ulster, editor of four collections of poetry and short stories for Portrush Writers.

I read Mary Farrell's *The Kingdom* with a sense of recognition and a sense of longing. For the world of the Kingdom is a sideways glance away, a step on an unknown path away, a sigh away. The language is our language, but again at a slant – youngling, birthing...

These tales of the inhabitants of The Kingdom are stories of love, of death, of storms and sadness. Tales of wandering and warmth and sometimes of failing to understand that difference is not always to be despised.

There is a basic acceptance that shelter and quiet and security are important, that a cottage is a nest. The people are close to nature, know how to use it for cures and healing. It is part of their 'life's weave' and perhaps it is the fact that we have distanced ourselves from what is natural that has closed us off from life in The Kingdom.

Maura Johnston, Author of Just Suppose 1999, The Whetstone 2019, From Aftergrass to Yellow Boots: A Glossary of Seamus Heaney's Hearth Language 2021

The Kingdom – Mary Farrell

To 'Gan' and Granda

~ who gave me my

Glens heritage ~

OTHER TITLES BY IMPSPIRED

Insaintity –
by J.L Christie

A Snowfall in Paris -
by Theresa C. Gaynord

A Bell in the Morning –
by Kevin McManus

Irish Hares & Seahorses -
by North Coast Writers

Poetland –
by Henry Bladon

They Move Away Like Waves –
by Mehreen Ahmed

Haiku Seasons –
by Jim Bates

Acknowledgements

By Mary Farrell

In the world of creative writing, it can be a spiraling journey to find the right Voice. Thankfully I had many companions who gave me wonderful directions enroute to The Kingdom.

Some of them came in group form, beginning with the friends I made in Flowerfield Arts Centre in 2017. North Coast Writers followed in 2019, along with Portrush Writers and This Writing Thing. These groups have been invaluable sounding boards, offering support and helpful advice. Other guidance came from individuals who delivered one-off Courses which provided flashes of welcome illumination. The many nudges along my path, given with kindness and generosity, were received with gratitude.

There were various enticing strolls down sideroads and cul-de-sacs on my journey. In the end however, I arrived at The Kingdom, a series of tales which, to me, still feel as if they are singing on their own. I am merely a recorder of their songs.

Thanks are due to two main editors, Bernie McGill and Kate Murphy. Anything I had transcribed with a heavy hand, they heard with a true ear, and their experience and expertise were much appreciated in The Kingdom, making it a more enchanting place.

Pat Cosgrave saw The Kingdom in her imagination and her sketches complement its Voice with her deft and delicate artwork.

Steve Cawte, the Editor of Impspired, trimmed its hedges and landscaped its valleys.

So many fellow-travellers! I am grateful to you all.

Welcome to The Kingdom.
Sit and read,
hear its Voice,
enjoy your stay.

Contents

Prologue

Made up of hills and valleys, it was not a large kingdom. The land was rich and green, its curves soft and blending, bordered on one side by the sea and on the other by low mountains. Over time, the inhabitants had developed their own ways and customs, not too dissimilar from those beyond the mountains, but different enough to be distinctive. They felt a kinship among themselves, like an echo deep in their birthing. To those outside the borders, they appeared fey, with an ability to connect with things unseen, a way of doing things which were not always explainable, an extra layer of knowingness. Those who lived there were not aware of this, thinking themselves to be just as normal as those foreign whom they met in the markets, or when they travelled to other lands. And yet it was there, deep in them but rarely surfacing, like a waft in the breeze or notes faintly heard from a pipe far away.

They lived their lives, as people do, with their share of joys and woes, curiosities and celebrations, and the comfort of routine.

And these are some of their tales.

Fighting the Good Fight

The sisters had clashed with sun-flare regularity. Chalk and cheese, they were - one Celtic fair, one Mediterranean dark, throwbacks to older genes. In nature too, so different. One, deeply sensitive, carried her wounds deep, gaining bitter strength from scratching at their memory. The other, volcanically dramatic, in anger would emit explosions of lava creating a nimbus of fire which would fade as quickly as it had flared and be forgotten even faster than that.

The jobbing worker came one potato digging to the farm in Glenfad. A bird of passage, with a soft southern lilt, golden tanned cheekbones and long hair braided back in a plait. Irresistible in his unselfconsciousness, he favoured neither one nor the other, engrossed in his picking at the earth, saying little, passing himself.

He must have been the only one who didn't see the signs, the hints, the siren calls. The sweet scent of camomile and rose hip, ribbons tied round necks and wrists, the intricate weaving of braids, the jostling for place at mealtimes, it all escalated. Everyone watched the play off, the build-up of luring snares, the unnecessary light touches, the hearts hung on sleeves, but he lived in his own world, hearing other songs, concentrating on picking and earning, counting down till his day of moving on.

"I'm thinkin' of asking him to stay on for the winter," the father confided to his wife. "A good worker, keeps his head down, does the work of two!" But the mother had been watching more closely than he, had been more aware of the drama on the stage, and knew in her bones there could be no good ending. Like all mother hens protective of her chicks, she started to talk him out of the idea. "We'll get by this winter on our own, and with one less mouth to feed, we could save a little and make an offer on O'Leary's field next spring." Blinded by land-lust, he came to agree as she pecked away at him.

On the day the boxes in the roof space overflowed with seed potatoes, the others having been stored or sold, the young man walked away down the lane, barely visible through the swirling shreds of tattered dreams. The father said loudly to his wife, "I wish you'd not talked me out of asking him to stay for the winter." The girls pivoted slowly towards each other, shared a long deep look, and then turned as one to dagger-eye their mother.

That winter, the mother passed a quiet, lonely, wordless time, the two girls got on like never before and their father beamed when O'Leary said yes to his offer on the field the next Spring.

The Changeling

The other siblings all slept in the fold-down settle bed by the fire, sardine-like, top to tail, but he slept in a straw-filled folded sheet, sewn together round the edges. It was softer for him… and safer. Many a bruise had been found in the morning among the other children due to a restless elbow jerked in hemmed-in sleep. Six children under nine, the O'Learys had listened to the thunderous sermons of the preachers – 'Go forth and multiply'- and had religiously done just that. But they had stopped when the sixth arrived, a month early.

No one had explained to Mrs O'Leary the effect of continual pregnancy, the steady leeching from her womb of her ability to breed. The first five were carbon copies of their father. Male or female, they were big-boned, ruddy faced, prodigious workers, hearty eaters - all cut from the same cloth. But though unaware of Darwinist theory, the family could see that the sixth was different. The template had weakened through overuse.

The doctor advised them to hand-feed him, as poor Mrs O'Leary, with five others to raise as well, now never seemed to have enough life force in her to produce the rich nourishing milk she had had for the others. So, he was different right from the start, causing extra work and trouble with his constant need for milk-soaked rags.

He grew slowly, but was thinner, quieter, parts of his skin almost translucent. His head seemed too heavy for his shoulders if he carried more thoughts, more knowledge than they... And when his hair grew long and ginger, not the trademark O'Leary black, that clinched it! He wasn't really one of them.

As he grew older, he seemed to become even paler, his eyes more piercing, his body more delicate. He listened with intensity. That made the boisterous O'Learys uncomfortable. Gradually they started to lower their voices around him or whisper behind his back. Unlike them he had not headed outdoors to the wide-open spaces of Glenbreen as soon as he could crawl. He didn't play their games, gambol round like large puppies as they did, laugh or smile much. He helped out in any way he could, but mainly indoors - with preparing the meals, tending to the fire, keeping the spartan home spotlessly tidy.

Eventually, after passing seven increasingly uneasy Springs, one morning he didn't wake up, leaving them without fuss or goodbyes. There was almost a sense of relief - no longer a cuckoo in the nest. The family burial plot was in the grounds of a ruined church on the hillside behind the house. He was buried there under a hawthorn tree.

They lived on in their routines but hadn't received his message. They hadn't seen their reflections in his large luminous eyes, didn't realise he had shown them how grateful they should be, for being one of the strong, full-of-life, earth-nourished O'Leary's. A precious chance given to them had been wasted. Shaped from a lighter cloth, he had shown them the strength and vitality of their life's weave. However, over time, their minds erased the memory of him in the same way the meadow grass smoothed out the outline of the tiny grave up on the hill.

Blessings Given

She'd always been a 'golden girl' right from birth, with flaxen hair which tousled in curls despite maternal brushing, and a wide smile in which even the coming and going of tooth-fairy gaps were charming. With a straight stare from eyes which echoed wide blue skies, she had an open way with her, never forward, never intrusive and listening just as much as she spoke. But it was more than that!

There appeared to be a glow about her, a pulsing of warmth, an aura of light which attracted people to her, in the same way they would instinctively move closer to a warm fire on a cold day. They were pulled, drawn, stroked and smoothed down by her. They would leave her side with reluctance, knowing that they were somehow now more nourished than they'd been before they'd met.

Her parents welcomed her birth and cherished her dearly, a lateling after many barren years. They would often agree with hindsight, she'd been well worth the wait. They felt well-compensated when eventually the womb, cradle and loft bed were in turn filled by her. At the small school midway up Glendora, she took care never to outshine the others. She singled out the saddened for comforting words, heartfully rejoiced with the small milestone victories of others, and in general lit up the world around her with peals of laughter, skipping steps and sparkling eyes.

But what was to become of her? In the way of things, it was expected that she would marry one day, but who was to be the blessed one? The males around her preened and jostled, proffered and strutted, clamoured for attention, but all were treated with gentle but definite equality. None were given special hope.

One day a new family came to the town at the shore, taking over the shop of a recently passed bachelor uncle. The father was a skilled shoemaker and thus warmly welcomed by the community. Boots and shoes could now be re-heeled and resoled instead of being replaced, saving precious coins needed elsewhere. But the shop had an added bonus.

As the townsfolk passed its open door, a wisp, a wave, a flow or sometimes a crescendo of notes would be heard, stirring their souls with beauty, raising their hearts and lightening their steps. Ethereal echoes of these sounds would swirl in their heads for many hours afterwards. How so?

It happened that the shoemaker and his wife had, among their three children, a boy who during his first exploring graspings as a toddler had lifted a wooden flute, given to his elder brother as a gift. From that first connection, it seemed to become part of him, an extension of his arm. Right from his first tentative playings and practicings, its notes seemed to yield all the beauty of the green glade from whence the wood for its carving had come. The essence of Nature at its richest would flood the hearts of any who heard the joyous lilt of boy and pipe.

His parents said it was his compensation, this ability not just to play but to enchant, for hadn't he been born blind. One gift not given at his conceiving, another given in his growing.

It was only natural that at some point in the flow of the Kingdom her shoes would need to be mended. Her clear gaze fell upon him by the fireside which he rarely left, unsure of movement in a world of unexpected obstacles and strange pathways. From then on, they were each other's completion. He was the only one who felt but did not see her warm glow. She was the only one who with her clear blue gaze saw the weave of the music in his soul, not just hearing it as others did. In time, they wed. From then on, every wedding, birthing, passing and celebration in the glen was enriched by the presence of them both, as she led him to whatever position in the gathering meant that all could see and hear them to their hearts' own contenting.

The Travelling Labourer

Such a great childhood he'd had growing up in the farm many miles to the south of the Kingdom. His Da had worked him and his two brothers hard, but also remembered from his own childhood that boys needed to play. Many hours were spent skimming stones on the sacred waters of the Holy Lake, swinging from natural curves in tree branches, walking all a-wobble along the tops of stone walls, arms outstretched for balance, to see who could get furthest. Yes, a happy childhood!

Though they both were careful not to let the others find out, he was his mother's favourite. From the far north-east, only leaving it after finding her husband-to-be among the guests at a family wedding, she was homesick for it - its people, its earth, and its ways. Seeing its echo most clearly in the genes of her eldest son, she would pour out her love for her homeplace to him when they were alone, and he felt its resonance in his soul. As he grew older, its hold on him deepened and flourished. Its magic crept into his soul and rooted there.

As he grew, it became obvious that he knew things that others did not. He'd know the very night a ewe was going to lamb, or the day the priest would make a visit, or what pig at market would turn out to be a sickly buy in the long run. His Da used this insight when it benefited his pocket, but it never sat well with him. "The Devil's work", he'd mutter under his breath. His wife had had the same feyness when they'd first met, but he'd long since put it out of her. At least he thought he had, for she'd simply learned to hide it from her superstitious, fearful spouse.

The boy was seventeen when his Ma first started to fail - stumbling when she carried a pail of water, dropping the armloads of wood she was bringing in for the fire, tearing apart the quiet of the night with her racking coughs. By the time he was eighteen she was bed-ridden, and they all knew she was not for this world much longer. His Da, a man of few words at any time, could not express his pain, growing more bloated with anger the thinner she became. When the time came to say private goodbyes to each, she told the boy to lift down a small cloth package from the top of the bedroom dresser.

"I want this to be yours, the only thing I have from my own place. The candle which burned bright during the Mass when the priest married us in the little church at the foot of the glen. I was given it to keep after the ceremony was over. It's a strange thing…"

She would've said more but a fit of coughing weakened her, and she fell back on the pillow, eyes closed. He tiptoed out with the package under his elbow, to give her time to strengthen to speak to the others.

Going outside, choked with the effort of holding back tears, he sat on a low stone wall waiting for the call that she was gone. Unwrapping the age-stained cloth, he stared at the candle - plain wax, about a foot long and an inch wide. Staring at it through blurred eyes, he imagined the ceremony - younger versions of his parents in love, the smell of incense, lilting Latin words, flickering candlelight. But wait now!... if it had burnt throughout the ceremony, then how come it was still full length and the wick was white! But at that moment of that thought, a roar of pain splintered the hush inside the cottage. His Da's voice. Whirling through the door, he threw the candle on the mantlepiece as he passed through to the single bedroom, now a death chamber.

After what seemed like an endless rosary said over the still form on the bed, he and Da rose stiffly from their knees. The second son had been sent for the priest and the youngest for Mrs Murphy, who traditionally did the laying-out thereabouts. Leaving the bedroom, in the kitchen they sat side by side, facing the beginning of their mourning together.

Suddenly… "What's that thing?"

His father pointed towards the candle half swathed in the cloth, still sitting on the mantelpiece. As he explained, his Da's face grew puce, and he seemed to swell like a toad.

"I told her years ago to get rid of that, it's a thing of the Devil. It moves on its own and won't go out."

He reached for it, but his son was quicker.

"No! It's the only thing she gave me. It's mine!"

"It's leaving this house now she's gone. If you're so set on keeping it, you can go too!"

This instant reply came not from the love in a father's heart but from a fear of his wife's otherness which had been barely contained in the man all his married years. A fear now unleashed in an anger which came from distorted grief.

"Out! Out now!"

The son and the candle were both tossed out the door, ending up lying on the path.

In that moment the son became a man, with a man's' choice before him. He could stay here, in due course inherit the farm. To do so he'd have to deny that part of him which was his mother, that otherness and feyness of hers which came from the north-east. He'd have the farm but only part of himself would be there to work it. He'd lose what he felt was the best part of his being, and betray his mother's memory.

Having made his choice, he stood up, picked up the candle and started off down the lane. His Da must have been watching. His father's own black coat and scarf were thrown out through the door, a paltry inheritance and far too big for him as his father was a tall man… but plainly it was to be all he'd get from him.

Broken-hearted and grieving, he turned his face to the north-east. He'd find work where he could in his homeplace. And in the strangest way, he felt he was walking into the arms of his inheritance from his mother.

Desires

She was the late child of elderly parents - a surprise arrival to them both. An eight-month sickly baby. Living high up Glenfad and being therefore remote from neighbours, they'd long since developed their own patterns, ways of living, loving, communicating together. They found it hard to adapt to a third. Their world was complete with only two, so she grew up feeling closed out, isolated from human connection. They were not unkind. She was fed, clothed, was taught what they knew, but growing up, she knew she was an extra, had not been wanted, felt insignificant in her everyday life.

This led to the growing of a deep burning fire in her, which strengthened with each year. She wanted to be important to someone, to come first, to be the centre of someone's world. Not in a selfish self-centred way. She didn't want the wide world to appreciate her, just one person would do. And as she got older and saw the ways of her culture, she realised that the best person to fulfil this need would be a husband.

She could never have been called pretty and being an eight-month baby had left her with a slight form, a straight back, a weak chest and poor eyesight for which she wore thick glasses. But anyone who bothered to spend time in her company would have realised that her isolation had made her sensitive and thoughtful, and thus kind beyond belief to the needs of others. Also, having been a sickly child herself, she became well versed in how to access nature's help to ease the symptoms of illness. Many who came to her door went away with goose grease for their chest or a woundwort paste for a cut. They didn't realise the pots also included a loving desire to ease pain coming from empathy and her open heart.

A final, practical, if opportunistic factor was that, as her parents were elderly, any future husband would not have too long to wait to inherit the homestead, not large but substantial enough not to be sneered at. And so, on reaching marriageable age, she looked around for eligible suitors down the Glen closer to the shore.

As soon as her eyes fell on Con Boyle whose father owned the local general store, her heart fell also, straight into love. He was not overly good-looking, but pleasant enough when she called for her groceries. He was the right age, and the Boyle family were known to be canny enough to appreciate a good deal when it was presented to them. An extra homestead would add to their coffers.

She took to shopping there more often than before, passing a little longer in conversation with him than was needed during purchasing, discreetly inquiring about his ways, his pastimes and most importantly, his routines. She needed to cross his path on a weekly basis to embed her presence in his consciousness. The more she learned of him, the more her heart was caught … and the more she wanted to be the one, the only one, for him.

Slowly, steadily, subtly she made progress. Until one Sunday afternoon he asked her to accompany him on a walk through Leanan Glen. Her gentleness soothed him. He asked again and over a few months it became a pattern. Her heart expanded with every walk. But then came the day that the niece of one of the families in the town visited from the far west.

At first most people were struck by her hair. A red head, not the usual dark of the Kingdom, and at first sight, that red overwhelmed all who met her. Waist length, curling in perfect tendrils, a living thing in itself as it flew and twirled and danced. It was many things to many people - the embers of the fire, the orange marigolds in the Rectory Garden, the copper in a rock, the setting of the sun. Each person saw their favourite thing and smiled. Later they realised that Roisin was also light of foot, with frequent tinkling laughter, creamy skin, and the joy of living in her eyes.

Con was blinded at first sight, and from then on, followed her like a puppy, until she agreed to marry him. His family also approved as they were prosaic about their marriage choices. She would be an asset serving in the grocery store. As for Roisin, Con adored her and let her be herself, running barefoot on the beach, getting up to watch the dawn, dancing as she cooked. He allowed her red-headed nature to blaze so she was content with a choice which nurtured her free soul. Her other suitors back home had been dour, wanting to harness her in their fields, taming her hair in the tight plait of the confining marriage they envisaged.

After congratulating Con and Roisin on their wedding day, the healer went back up the glen to her parents' farm, which she rarely left again. An arrangement was made with a neighbour to do the weekly shopping, take the animals to market, and other such practical things. After her parents died in their own time, within a couple of months of each other as they would have wished, she was only seen by those who went for their healing jars, still freely given but now just containing ointments. Some say that they saw her from time-to-time walking at midnight through Leanan Glen, but sure, why would she be doing that?

The Oak

There was a tree in Dara Glen, just at the side of the road leading to the main market town. Beauteous it was, thick of core, deep of root, splendid in its strength with the branches evenly spaced, growing ever leafier with each Spring. It was an oak, old of knowing, protective of wisdom, and revered by all those of the Kingdom who passed it daily, or by those going to or from the fortnightly markets. Many had sat at its base sheltering, they said, from the sun or rain. In truth the tree connected with them, grounded them, wrapped around them.

Many situations were perceived more clearly, many plans of action decided upon under its whispering boughs, but only for those born in the Kingdom. For those from outside, it was indeed a magnificent tree. But for those who lived there, the right decisions about family, about the land, about their future could safely be made in its shelter. It eased the way for those of the Kingdom to become aware of their own inherent knowledge - who to marry or leave, when to travel in order to grow and learn, or how to accept changes in their world such as the death of a loved one or the empty nest of a child moved on. The leaves would murmur, the boughs would sway, and the smell of the sap would grow stronger. With the grassy earth softening beneath them, answers would appear and root in all who questioned. The space beneath the oak leaves enabled their souls to whisper to them. Although they did not speak of it among themselves - those of the Kingdom never needed to speak of such things - a knowingness in them recognized the power of the tree's shelter, and they sought it out when they needed wisdom.

Then came the summer of the Great Storm. Days and days of heavy heat following each other, the pressure continued to layer until it all exploded one night in a blast of power. Shards of lightening, explosions of thunder and finally, mercifully, a sheet of heavy raindrops fell, much needed to nourish the dry earth. When the folk of the Kingdom came out the next morning to feel the freshness of the air, they were stunned into silence and became still. One of the lightning shards had hit the oak. Two-thirds of its semicircle of branches was still untouched, but there on the ground lay the other third, seared at its end by the fire which had ripped it from its body.

A scar on the main trunk showed where Nature had carried out its amputation. The branches at the top of the oak seemed to lean over the severed remains on the earth below as if in sadness, gently drooping, trembling with soft sighs of mourning. All day long small groups - individuals, families, friends - came to pay their respects, their shock evident, their grief deep, silent as they stared a homage to the tree's loss. As they turned to walk away, their shoulders sagged as if they carried the weight of the space which had been left.

By the next day however, after a sleepless night, one man had birthed an idea. He went from door to door telling of his plan which was greeted with relief by all. The general unease started to lift. Neil Og, as he was commonly known, the most skilled carpenter in the Kingdom, had now a drive - a calling it felt so strong - to take the fallen branches and from them, carve what would be his life's masterpiece. A bench of such comfort and beauty that all who sat there would be eased and restored, would become clear minded and resolute. It would be placed under the arc of the oak in the space where the branches had been, so the tree could still work its magic and whisper answers.

All that long winter, he toiled and carved and polished and shaped. The next Mayday, his creation, unseen by any until then, was carried out in procession on the shoulders of the leading menfolk of the town. Laid with great respect on the green sward specially flattened for it, it was positioned with its back to the trunk of the oak, whose scar had faded during the greening of that spring. There were those who would swear till their deathbed that, at that moment, they heard the tree sing at the reunion.

From that day on, in the way of the Kingdom, life continued as before in Dara Glen, with passers-by coming to the seat in pilgrimage when they needed heartsease or answers or simply just peace. For their part, Neil Og, and all the future generations of his family, who came to be affectionately known as the Bench Keepers, repaired and cared for it when the tree called them to do so.

For its part, the tree continued to nourish just as it always had.

The Power of the Spoken Word

She couldn't remember when it first began, when she first noticed the 'effect'. She'd always been wary since she learnt how to speak, of using people's first names. The visiting missionary said that in Africa, the natives didn't like their photograph taken as they felt it robbed them of a little bit of their souls. She understood that. Each time she called people by their first names, she could see them become a little lighter skinned, a little more see-through.

So, at a very early age, she stopped using first names altogether, and developed ingenious ways of getting round this. Within her immediate family, they lived on top of each other in the little cottage in Glenfad, and so rarely used each other's names anyway. If she had to travel further afield and be in a group at a bigger family gathering, at the monthly market, or at some other social occasion, "How's himself today?" she'd say ……or she'd refer to "the little one" or "your brother". Most people didn't notice……. but a few did.

For example, the Murphys had moved in just down the glen to a two-room cottage just like theirs. She'd begun playing with Aileen, who was the same age as her. The only worry about this new friendship was that from time to time, as she was enjoying it so much, she'd forget herself and call her new friend by her first name. Aileen was fair of skin to start with, creamy without freckles or marks. After a few months of roaming the fields together, lying in the grass looking at the clouds, plaiting reeds to make dolls, Aileen began to develop an ethereal sheen, her cheeks, arms and legs glowing with translucence.

Great Aunt Murphy, who was wise in the ways of medicine and knew a great many cures, told her parents to send her for a few months to stay with their cousins on their farm some distance away outside the Kingdom to see if the clear mountain air there would make any difference. And it did! She came back as hale and hearty and full faced as she'd ever been, but after a few more months of running the hills with her friend, the noticeable fading started again. The Murphys held a family conference and decided to move for good to another cottage beside their cousins. The family farm there was a goodly size, and they could always do with a few more hands… and wasn't it worth it for the good of Aileen's health. And so, they left, and the girls never saw each other again. That cottage was taken over by two elderly sisters who kept to themselves and spoke to few.

Left behind, at the age of eight she was brought to the May hiring fair by her father and taken on by a childless couple who lived high up in the next glen, Glenard. They were getting on in years and needed someone to do the heavier lifting of the water and wood, the sacks and sheaves. She was young, but cheap enough for them. She thrived. They were fair to her, demanding a day's work but giving a day's bed and board, and she was always able to call them just "Missus" and "Sir". One autumn, a jobbing labourer from south of the Kingdom came to stay for a month to help with the potato picking. He too kept to himself, sleeping in the outside lean-to but she had to go and call him in three times a day from the field for his food. Tanned when he arrived, each week he paled a little, but he'd no time or inclination for looking in mirrors, and the elderly couples' rheumy eyes couldn't register any change, so only she noticed it. She was relieved when he moved on after the field was picked clean.

After two years up the high valley, the "Missus" died of a consumption and "Sir" went to live with his brother in the west. Now a strong and wiry ten, her family found work for her in Boyles' General Store in the shore town at the foot of Glenfad. She slept in the attic and worked in the shop all day for her food and clothes. The wages went directly to her family each month. Here it was also possible to avoid the "effect" most of the time. She'd wrap up goods, deliver them or clean up the shop . She was never expected to use a first name, only full titles. What shop underling would do anything else!

But from time to time she'd forget herself in conversation, let a name slip. Certain customers began to avoid her, asking if they could be served by someone else. They couldn't put their finger on it, but she made them feel uncomfortable, almost vulnerable, almost thinner-skinned. Well, the Boyles couldn't be having it- whatever it was that was happening, They might begin to lose customers. A long conference was held with her parents, which of course resolved nothing, as after all they were not the ones who knew what was happening.

It fell to her to come up with her own solution,

which pleased everyone else but kept her secret safe. She declared that she'd been thinking long and hard about it for many months and had decided that she had a vocation to be a nun. The order she wished to join was the Carmelite Monastery of the Nativity, many days' journey away in the south-west, a silent order in which she would never speak again. Her family was overjoyed that one of their own had chosen to represent them in the church and with God. The Boyles were delighted that they would lose no more customers, and now had the name for being a saintly business at which to apprentice young ones.

However, when the Convent door closed behind her, and her hair was shaven and she was dressed in a habit, although she knew her secret was now safe and she'd never be cast out as evil, she also knew that she'd never speak again in her life. At that moment her heart and soul started to shrivel and wither, and the essence of her slowly started to die.

Lead Kindly Light

JohnJo had been born high up at the top of Glenard. His was not a bad life - a roof over his head, a family who loved him, food to eat, if plain, but a life socially isolated. Reaching the age where he was expected to find a wife, he had begun to long for his heart to be held and his soul soothed.

However, romance would not be found in the fields or on the hills, but at the regular fortnightly dances held in the Church Hall eight miles away. Sixteen miles had to be walked there and back on the search for his Grail, but he was stoical and realistic, knowing that it would take time and stamina until he found the right bride. Strengthened by field work and driven by necessity, he would make that walk for as long as it took, but one thing did disquiet him - the dark.

He knew the pathway well - it was the one they walked on the way to market - but the dark filled the landscape with distorted shapes. The family had no money to spare for lantern oil or torches of any other kind. So twice a month he made the long dark journey, walking on his own, talking sense into himself that there was nothing out there harmful or bad, real or fanciful.

Having braved the journey, each month he would dance, watching the young girls of the Kingdom birl and skip before him like a flock of starlings. And each month he would add brush strokes to the image of the kind of wife who would suit him best. Then one night on the way home, deep in thought about what had just happened at the dance, he saw a dark form on the path before him. Gathering up his courage, he walked even faster to catch up. If it was going to be a dangerous encounter, he'd rather know sooner than later. Already tired, he wasn't going to leave the well-trodden path to circumvent the figure, even if he could move faster or break his way through the thick bushes on either side of the way ahead.

As he caught up, the figure moving ahead of him revealed itself to be a that of a tall man, in a full-length black topcoat, collar pulled up round his ears. He had also wrapped a black scarf round the bottom half of his face as protection from the cold. His stride was long and steady, surefooted and even.

"Hey there!" JohnJo shouted, much relieved to find it was another man and not some creature from his own worse fears.

"Can I walk along with you?"

The figure started a little, as if he had been lost in his own thoughts, unaware of another coming up behind him.

Unwinding the scarf in order to speak, he replied in a deep voice, "Certainly, I should be glad of company on this lonely trek."

Together they walked on side by side. Introducing themselves, JohnJo explained he was coming from the dance. The stranger explained that he had been to the town to visit a friend who had been taken ill but now seemed to be on the mend.

Soon into the conversation JohnJo referred to his fear of the dark, whereupon the stranger reached deep into a pocket in his voluminous coat. He pulled out a long candle and matches. Breaking the candle in two, he handed one half to JohnJo and then lit both segments.

Much relieved by this unexpected and welcome gift, JohnJo went to move forward, the candle in his hand, but was stopped by the stranger.

"No, put the candle down on the ground... slightly in front of you but to the side," the deep voice instructed, "and then walk on."

Taken by surprise, he was told without question, and was amazed to find that as he moved forward, so did the candle. It seemed to hover about a foot above the earth, never veering from the path, the flame always steady, illuminating the way clearly. The stranger had done the same with his half.

"But how…?"

"Do not ask!" ordered the stranger, so Johnjo did not, not wanting to lose the light as much as he didn't want to annoy the stranger. There was no more conversation.

This strange situation continued until JohnJo reached his father's farm, stopping to turn in at the gateway. At that point the stranger bent down, lifted both halves of the candle, which curiously had not burnt down, blew out the flames and put the two halves back in his pocket. He then rewound his scarf around his head.

"Goodnight. Pleasure to have had your company".

And before JohnJo could say anything in reply, he strode off into the night, continuing along the now pitch-black path.

Although he often wondered about the uncanny events of that night, and who the stranger was, and how the candles had moved and burned, JohnJo soon had other things to think about as that was the last of those dances he ever had to attend. He had made arrangements earlier that night. On the following Sunday he would go to a local farmer and ask him if the elder of his lovely dark-haired full-o-life O'Leary daughters could become his wife. As indeed she did!

Beyond the Shop

Now that Kevin Boyle had given up the running of the shop at the shore and turned it over to his son Con, he was bewildered. He'd walk down the street and people would say to him, "Sure and aren't you having a grand time, now you're retired!" He'd nod and smile back and wonder what was wrong with him that he wasn't. No, he was not having a grand time!

At first, he'd thought that he'd pass a few hours each day in the shop just helping out, but it soon became obvious that that wouldn't work. Con felt he was interfering. His son's new wife, Roisin, had some mad ideas which annoyed him. "Times of the Year" she called them, putting out to the front goods for St Patricks Day or Easter or the start of the school holidays. She said it put people in the mind to buy things, but he thought it was nonsense. People had always known what they wanted. Everything in the shop had always had its own place so customers knew where to find it. All this moving about of stock unsettled him to the point where he preferred now to avoid the shop when he could. It annoyed him even more that sales had slowly crept up since he'd left, something he didn't want to think about.

What one and all but himself could plainly see was that he needed a wife to fill the emptiness at his side and the emptiness in his life. He'd always been fond of female company. Reared as the only boy with five sisters accounted for that. He had mourned his wife's death for many years, when she died giving birth to Con. It had been a good marriage. At first a practical one between friends but one which then had grown into a deep love. Her going left a space which he had been unable to fill.

He talked with ease to his female customers, some of whom lingered long over their purchases. He didn't even register their interest blinded by the misconception that he could maybe fill the gap in his life with longer hours, harder work at the shop. Now the shop was gone, he walked holes in his shoes, tramping the same pathways the length and breadth of Glenfad. He bought many books which he started but never finished. He confirmed what he had always suspected: that he was not a natural drinker. He liked to go to the pub only on the third Thursday of every month, when he knew it would be full. Various local musicians gathered there on that particular night… as would many who wanted to listen to them.

And then a new resident came to the area. A canny woman, she'd the situation well measured only a few months after moving back to the Kingdom from the south. She'd lived there till her husband died seven years ago. Since then, she felt she'd spent enough time touring round visiting the children and grandchildren, and far far too much time rattling around in a house which was too big for her to clean, let alone live in.

She'd felt the tendrils of her homeplace reach out to her heart, heard the siren call of the soft hills and the lilting tongue of her own folk. The pull became too strong… and back she'd come. The little cottage she bought on the edge of the town at the Glen foot fitted neatly around both her and the precious things she'd brought back from the south. At night, in her bed, she heard the same sounds she'd heard as a child - the mating cries of the owls, the "mirr" of the sheep, the slurring of the shingle on the shore. She slept deep and well and dreamed sweet dreams.

As she watched him pad past her door each day on his walk towards the promenade, each day his shoulders lower and his heart a little more shrivelled, deep within she realised that he needed her. She also realised she'd be well content if she came to his aid. First, she made sure that, thanks to small town gossip, he knew all about the seed and breed of her, and her past story. Then interchanges of "Good morning" and "Fine day" increased between them as their paths chanced to cross.

One morning, she timed it that she was coming out through her small front gate just as he was passing… and didn't she trip. With a small cry of pain, she sank to the ground, dropping her empty shopping basket. Well trained by his sisters and by his late wife, and naturally chivalrous and kindly, he stepped forward with speed… and just the right amount of respect for her lost dignity in falling. Having established that she'd done nothing more than turn her ankle on an uneven paving stone, he held her arm as she limped her way back into the cottage, and then sank onto the yielding sofa in her small front room.

"The doctor?" he queried, but she reassured him that she'd be fine with just some rest and quiet, though a cup of restorative tea would be very welcome. It was duly made, delivered and drunk. It seemed natural to him that he'd call the next afternoon to check on her progress. He'd walked far up the glen that morning to get a jar of the soothing ointment from the healer who lived up there. He trusted her skills. After all, she'd nearly married his son. Of course, while he was relating the story of that courtship, he made a cup of tea for them both. And any kind Samaritan would then have to check daily on her improvement.

As the ankle settled, so too did the pattern of afternoon calls. During each visit the soothing conversation of things past and present flowed and ebbed between them, in the way of the tides on the shore outside. The neighbours watched, nodded their heads, approved - with the odd female exception. Con and Roisin felt a burden lift from them as they saw his shoulders straighten. The next Easter Tuesday, at the wedding, the church was packed with both family and friends who truly wished them well. Many knew that she had spent her years in the south teaching dancing as a pastime while her husband had worked, but only she knew as she walked up the aisle that she was still as sure-footed as any goat on the hills.

The Inheritance

It was a curious situation, the only one of its type so far in the lawyer's long career. An elderly hermit of a bachelor, who had died leaving a goodly farm high up in Glenorlar, had left a very detailed will. The farm was to go to whoever of his next of kin had a certain set of specific characteristics. Without these, the inheritance would bypass all other family members and the farm would go to the young labourer who had helped him run the farm in his later years. The old man had been determined about this. This particular beneficiary would only be found through a diligent - and thus lucrative - search by the law firm. The farmer had given the firm any family papers he'd had but did not know of any cousins or other family members still alive. All the kin he knew of belonging to him had died many years since. He'd made his wishes very clear a few years ago when the will was being drawn up, probably the last time he'd been away from the farm.

"Well, that's what the will says, apart from a few minor details which can only be dealt with when I find out the intentions of the beneficiary."

The lawyer let his face fall back into its usual relaxed form. He settled back as comfortably as he could on the hard, upright chair in the Mother Superior's Parlour, folding his hands together on his well-established rounded stomach. The legal search had led him here to a Carmelite Convent in the far west. There had been a daughter born to a second cousin, and though there'd been some talk of her being strange in some way, she'd been accepted here six years ago as a novice. She was here beside him now, standing just inside the door, a quiet figure in the full robes of the novitiate, head down, eyes lowered

His stomach rumbled. He loved his food, though here in the Convent little he'd got but a cup of watery tea. Still, it appeared he wouldn't have to stay long. This was a straightforward visit. He 'd soon be left and tucking into a tasty dinner in the hotel before setting off the next day, back home to the Kingdom in the north-east.

He was somewhat surprised to be there at all, if truth be told. He'd thought a man wouldn't get into a convent of nuns who didn't speak, that they would insist that he'd have to deal with a go-between of some sort. But the old farmer had left strict instructions that a story and a special message had to be delivered in person to whoever would inherit the farm. If not, the whole will would be null and void. Then the farm would go to the state without any fee for the firm. A strange request, but maybe the whole family had been a bit 'touched' by the sound of it. Anyway, it had given him a jaunt to the west, with a few good hotel dinners on the journey.

Therefore, he'd made it very clear in his letter to the Mother Superior that he had to speak to the novice, face to face, and pass on the message. No fool he, he suspected the same Mother Superior would soon make plans for any money coming from the sale of a farm, of whatever size and however far away. She had indeed, despite the usual rules of the Order, agreed to the meeting of the unlikely trio now in her parlour. The three facing each other were herself, the somewhat rounded and determined legal gentleman, and the beneficiary, a few weeks short of her eighteenth birthday.

The lawyer had been surprised at her lack of reaction to his announcement of the contents of the will. She'd inherited a farm after all! But he just assumed that, as she was about to be fully ordained in a few weeks' time, her vocation was so strong that such worldly things no longer held any interest for her.

"Let's get this over and done with then. Tell the old man's story, give the message and get back in time for a nap before eating"

He had begun to salivate at the idea of the roast lamb the hotel was serving for dinner that night…..and so he began to relate his tale.

In the old man's youth, he'd fallen deeply in love with a fair lass from a neighbouring farm. Coming eighteen she was, with emerald eyes, a spring in her step and a laugh which warmed his heart and lifted his soul. Following custom, he went to her father to ask for her hand. The reply shattered his world forever. On her eighteenth birthday she was to be married to the widower who owned the next-door farm, thus doubling the size of both. Never mind that the widower was over thirty years older than her, and that she herself had not yet even been told. It had all been arranged, was set in stone. Anyway, there were plenty of other lasses who would suit him just as well, he was told.

But there weren't... and he never married. He held just one flame all his life, trying never to think of her married to the elderly widower. When the time came to make his will, he determined to do what he could to ensure this same tragedy never happened to another. His farm was to go outright to the female relative of his who was closest to her eighteenth birthday. She could then, as a woman of independent means, make a free choice of whom she wished to spend her life with... or even remain alone if she wanted. The message to be relayed from the old man to the young girl were the words, 'Enjoy your freedom to choose'.

The cynical lawyer had, to his own surprise, been touched by this tale and the old man's gesture, which was probably why more energy had been put into fulfilling the requests of the will than the fee merited. He'd even been a little dismayed when it was revealed that the girl had already chosen to spend her life in a convent - but such was the way of things! Everything possible had been done to honour the old man's wishes. No reaction was expected from the stern-faced Mother Superior – he suspected that any empathy for human love had dried up in her these many years - but he thought the tale might have affected the young girl in some way.

But she didn't react to the story, had remained silent, eyes down, barely rustling her robes when she breathed. Seconds passed in silence when suddenly a thought occurred to him.

"She's only young and might be worried about how to manage a farm on her own. Of course! What a fool I've been not to think of that before now!" he chided himself.

He rushed to elaborate. The old man had had a helper for the last years of his life, who lived in a separate lean-to attached to the farm cottage. In reality, the young man had increasingly run the farm by himself as the old man's bones had aged and stiffened. He was more than capable of continuing to manage it, and indeed would prefer to do so as he would find it hard to find a place elsewhere. You see, he was born deaf. The old man had deliberately taken him on because of his desire for peace and quiet in which to think his own thoughts. He wanted a farmhand, not conversation, and so the helper had taken over more and more of the running of the farm, learning its ways. By the end, even the need for gestures between them waned, and they saw each other little during the day.

"Would this make any difference to a future decision about the farm?" the novice was then formally asked. As his words faded in the air, the girl changed before their very eyes. Surprised they watched her back straighten, her shoulders rise and level out. She moved a few steps forward, her head lifting ever so slowly.

"Thank you, oh thank you!" she whispered in a voice unfamiliar with speaking.

However, the most startling thing for the two in the Parlour was the blazing light which now beamed from her beautiful huge emerald eyes, inherited from her grandmother.

The Ember

She had been walking forever. Green as the grass was, soft as the hills curved, plentiful as the earth creatures and birds continued to be, she was so tired of being on the move. She was slight and lithe and fit, with a good eye and the stillness and instincts of a natural hunter, and so was rarely hungry but still was always just on the under-edge of feeling stomach-full. She wanted to stop running. She wanted a home. She wanted to be loved and cherished as she had been when she was young, so short a time ago.

She, her mother and three siblings had lived with the branch of the O'Leary family who farmed in Glenfad, sleeping at night in their lean-to. She had never known her father, but her mother was a good worker on the farm, doing her share. That had secured their home, though they were all expected to work for their keep. There was no leeway for a lazy or slow worker.

She was totally black, or so she thought! If she'd been able to see under her chin, there was a small cluster of white hairs, a little tuft of light in the rich velvet dark of her coat. She'd been happy for the six months she was on the farm with her mother and the other kittens. Then came the August Fair and off Colm O'Leary went, to sell the extra sheep, buy what was needed for the autumn, and meet up with his friends.

As expected, he came back a different man. As usual, after he'd done his business, he sought out his cronies. Down the path they went behind the church and out came the poteen. Too much of it never sat well with him. Everyone knew to stay out of his way, both on his return when the devils were first in him, and then during the next day when he suffered the aftermath of them leaving.

On this evening, though successful at market, he'd a bee in his bonnet, a sting from his cousin Niall. There were too many animals living off his back on the farm, contributing nothing. He rampaged around the barn looking for the cats to drown them in the burn.

'Good for nothings. Only need one! The mother's enough!", the drink in him snarled.

The cats scattered, started to run. When her panic finally ebbed, she was in unfamiliar territory, too lost to find a way home. Her life of being on the move had begun. Living off the land, but still always harking back to the rest and comfort and security she'd known.

One night she sheltered in an empty rabbit hole in a ditch. At first light, just as she was gingerly peering out into the dawn's mist she heard the firm step of a woman, her long skirts swishing among the herbs she wanted to gather while they were at their freshest in the morning dew. This was when they were at their best for the making of healing pastes and salves.

The kitling tried to duck back, but too slow, too late! Sharp eyes had seen her.

"What have we here?" said a voice, slightly hoarse as if too rarely used.
A long -fingered hand reached in, pulled her out, held her at arms-length to have a good look ....

and then the strangest exchange occurred.

Two sets of fear and fatigue and loneliness crossed over, from one to the other. Each soul keened 'I don't want to be alone' and heard its echo.

After what was only a moment but seemed like an age, a small ember began to shine and grow in the core of each of them. The little black cat, held close and already inevitably named Shadow, nuzzled into the neck of the slight lady in black. With each stride back towards the small farm, which was in future to be their joint home, the purring got louder and louder and louder. The woman's mouth curved in an unfamiliar shape but one which was to be seen there often in the years ahead.... a smile!

The Path Appearing

Owen Murphy was seventeen, and as near to being a man as you can be while still living at home. His family were close not cloying, supportive not strangling, respectful not repressive. But growing up in Glenorlar had been easy for him anyway as he was the second son, not the one predestined to take over the farm. He hadn't grown up with the weight of responsibility regarding a pending inheritance. He was skilled round the farm, could turn his hand to almost anything, but was aware enough to know he was a Jack of all trades but Master of none. This was why he had not gone the route of a trade, having no one particular skill to be honed and shaped in the long hard firing of a seven-year apprenticeship. The general day-to - day life of a farm suited him, with its work dependent on the turning of that year and laid out within the scaffolding of the seasons and the moon's arc. Planting, tending, nurturing, harvesting, storing - that cycle suited and nourished him.

However, he felt he would soon need to choose his own life-path. His family and the farm had moulded him, had taught him *who* he was, but he could feel the urge growing to declare *what* he was. He knew himself to be capable but not creative enough to build from scratch, responsible but not rebellious enough to throw down his glove at a new challenge. Self-aware indeed, but he was not yet ready to fully face the world in which he lived and gouge out a new curve in it, creating for himself a design for going forward.

So often throughout that year of his life, he would go to his special place, a large flat grey rock overhanging a crossroads high up in the glen. There he would try to peer ahead through the mists of the future to see which path to follow… but nothing ever appeared. However, he was not the type to be anxious, knowing that in the way of the Kingdom, his road would emerge when the timing was right. And of course, that was indeed the way of it.

That May, his Da came home from the Hiring Fair, with the news that an elderly farmer, even higher up the same glen, was looking for a helper to run his place, as he felt the ache in his bones growing ever stronger and he was able to do less and less. If the candidate suited, the old farmer would be content enough for someone to eventually take over the running of his farm completely. No one at the Fair had been keen as the place was too quiet for them. Rarely a human voice was heard there, the old man being a recluse, the neighbours few and distant and passers-by non-existent.

Da and he tramped up the hill the very next day. After a short but pointed conversation between his Da and the old man about duties, payment and the degree to which the old man didn't want to be disturbed, all was settled. The next Sunday he carried his small bag of private possessions on his back up the glen and set it in the lean-to beside the barn. He spent the evening walking round assessing what needed to be done, drawing up in his head a future daily routine of chores. Before going to bed, he shared a silent cup of tea with his new master. Both slept well. The farmer was content his farm was now in good hands. He'd have little to do on it in the future but live out his days quietly in peace. The lad was content that indeed, the Kingdom - with a little help from his Da - had provided the perfect niche for him. A farm to run, a place to feel at home where it didn't matter that he could hear nothing, as he had been deaf since birth.

Over the following years, the old man increasingly settled in his chair by the fire in winter and in the one by the door in summer, leaving the running of the farm to the lad who became a broad-shouldered capable manager, needing no direction in what was best for the good of the animals or the wants of the land. In time, even the few gestures used at first faded almost completely away, the two living side by side in peace and quiet. Each did what suited him best, thinking his own thoughts. They ate in silence the morning porridge and the evening stew prepared by the young man. They slept in their separate snugs, one in the cottage, the other in an adjoining room which had been built in place of the original lean-to.

In the due course of time, one morning the old man was found still and unwaking, a gentle smile on his wrinkled features. A few days later a lawyer, aided by the familiar gesturing and hand movements of his father, asked the young man to stay on until the will and the future of the farm was sorted. He was content to do so, confident that as a satisfying path had been found for him once, a second one would also appear. As indeed it did.

A young woman, or more correct to say a lass

barely eighteen, was to inherit. She was coming there to live but needed the manager to stay on. She too, it was implied rather than declared outright, was as reticent about talking as the old man had been. She was rumoured to be independent and strange in her ways. It was obvious that she didn't care that there would be those in the glen who would gossip. A young girl and a single manager in his late twenties alone on the same farm! Well! He was just glad he wouldn't have to leave the place which had become his home, and the care of the animals and the land which had become his life.

His trust and confidence in the Kingdom's power to create the right way for him, was rewarded on the day she arrived. In the few steps from the cart to the farm doorway, a sudden impish breeze blew her shawl back, unmasking a head strangely shaven of hair. A pale but beautiful face was revealed, with emerald eyes which blazed with joy. Her whole body radiated delight in its freedom of movement. Her being pulsed with the beat of life flowing. All this he glimpsed, felt, absorbed before she disappeared through the doorway… but that was enough. In that moment he realised he was the one chosen to be here specially for her, to protect and care for her for as long as she needed him. He also knew that his path had been revealed to him, to follow with trust, loyalty and love.

Smiles

The three might have looked out of place elsewhere but seemed aptly fitted for that moment, for that space in Leanan Glen, all of them in black, all with their heads covered in shawls. The eldest was slightly stooped of shoulder, but still slender of body, white hair visible under her shawl. The second was also slim, but that may have come from hard work, if the calluses on her hands and the dirt under her fingernails were anything to judge by. Although probably only in her forties, the shadow in her face made her look older. Premature grey showed in the dark wisps of hair which escaped from her bun and curled around her face. The third was the youngest by far, with still a hint of the plumpness of her teenage years upon her, still a swirl of youth about her form. Her hair was raven dark, with tendrils of shiny curls which burst from her shawl and nestled on her shoulders.

They each carried a bunch of wildflowers, freshly picked on the way to the grave. After a few minutes standing there, they placed them down in turn, eldest first, on the mound in front of them. Its six feet by three-feet grassy plot bore a circle of grey stones in which was laid a cross of smaller white stones from the shore. There'd been no money for a proper stone memorial, so they'd improvised. Also in the grey circle, in even smaller white stones, was marked out the name, Johnjo O'Kane. They came every year on that day - in kinship to that spot - to honour, to remember, to re-connect.

The mother remembered the day of his birth, a second labour easier than the first. She felt she must have walked the length of the Kingdom round and round the cottage, the pains coming quicker and quicker. Some instinct in her acknowledged the natural way of this. She'd not had that freedom with the all-important first-born, the heir. The wise woman had been called to her then, insisting she stay propped up in the cottage's only solid bed, drinking bitter potions to ease the labour. This time she'd insisted that she didn't need the wise woman. All was well, she just knew it. You see, this baby was, from the start, to be for her, just for her. The elder had been for the family, to hold the land, to keep the name, to continue the line. But this one would be her lamb, bonding with her like with no other family member, filling a special spot in her heart.

She remembered the few days after his birth when she was allowed the luxury of staying in bed, before returning to the life of the farm. There he lay in the bed with her, in the crook of her arm, sleeping his peaceful sleep as she nuzzled his soft head, smelling the special baby smell of him. He was so good, this babe of her core.

And she smiled at that memory, and it warmed her heart.

The second of the trio remembered their courtship, meeting for the first time at the fortnightly dance. She'd known he'd been watching her for a few weeks before he came over. Hadn't she been one of the dark-haired O'Leary girls, attracting a host of suitors, both suitable and not. All were lured into her circle by the life which sparked from her, and the laughter which enslaved. He'd been wary and respectful, almost expecting to be by-passed. It was this very hesitance which snared her. She'd had enough of the confident bucks who saw only the sheen of youth, and who might become accustomed too quickly to ownership after exchanging rings. With him she felt she'd be a prize he'd value as long as he lived.

And so, he did, until the day when the pony slipped on the mucky slabs. A wheel long overdue for fixing broke under the sudden swerve. In his fall from the front seat of the cart, his head unexpectedly hit the ground at the wrong angle… and he was instantly gone. But not before she'd had many years of affectionate touchings and kind words and private smiles and safe sleeping with him in the bed, held by his arms, breathing in his smell and contentedly listening to his gentle night noises.

And she smiled at that memory, and it warmed her heart.

The daughter remembered her Da from the first memory she ever had, sweeping her off the ground in a great high arc. She knew he'd never let her drop. She was his sweeting, the only girl after four boys. While the boys were needed to work on the farm, she was the most precious gift his wife could have given him, or so he often told the both of them. The liveliest sound on the farm was the two of them laughing, the differing tones and sounds and depths, his deep and hearty, hers tinkling and full of joy.

She saw every market sitting astride his shoulders, was at every selling and buying of a beast, and passed every family wedding and funeral with her hand in his. He loved the boys and her Ma, but these two were part of the other. They all knew it… and all accepted it without envy. It was simply the way it was. She was still too young when he left her, but the memories were so many, so intense, so personally hers, she knew she had been given a glimpse of her future husband because only one like him would do. Hadn't he told her so one special Sunday afternoon together?

And she smiled at that memory, and it warmed her heart.

The time came, as it always did, when they all turned as one and made their way back to the farm, the smiles staying on their lips, each quiet with their own memories. Even from beyond, the part that JohnJo had played in his womenfolk's' lives strengthened and nourished them, as he had always intended it would.

Knowing

All her young life, as far back as anyone could recall, she'd had a way with animals, wild or tame, but especially with horses. First thing every morning, it was always she who took the pony down to the pool, where the burn fell into a round bowl in the earth, formed in a time before time. There the pony would slake its thirst, while she cleaned its coat with a badger hairbrush, dipped in the clean clear shining water. Rhythmic and hypnotic it was, and both she and the pony loved this time each day. Her father, seeing her content, indulged her, giving her extra time away from the farm chores. Anyway, when he travelled the roads of Glendora or went to market, didn't everyone say, "Ah Caitlin's a great hand with that pony. Doesn't it look grand, good enough for the gentry!" and he'd bask in the reflected glow of her grooming.

It was a lovely spot, the pool low in the glade, the trees greeting each other overhead. The light dappled through their leaves onto the surface of the water, silvered by its cold inflow from a stream formed high in the glen. The only sounds were the joyful notes from the birds in the branches, the occasional snort of bliss from the pony and the tinkle of the water from time to time as it moved with a wind blow or a leaf fall.

As the only person who normally went there, she

was surprised one morning when they arrived to find a stranger sitting on a poolside rock, strangely still, staring at the water. Dark haired and dark eyed he was, with a mane of lush thick locks spread over his shoulders, a fine well-built torso, and long long legs tucked in below him. At the same time both were startled, both began to speak, both laughed as they hesitated. Then from this jerky start a conversation began to flow. He told of how he was a travelling worker, originally from the isles to the north, working his way round the kingdom, mainly from smithy to smithy as he'd a natural gift in working with metal. As he spoke, with the hint of a soft burr, she looked deep into his eyes, and felt the heart and soul of her move towards him. Coming to herself with a start after about an hour, she remembered the pony, the farm chores, her waiting father, and rose reluctantly to leave with a "Will you be back here again?" bursting from her as she made to leave the pool.

"Indeed, and every morning for some time," came the reply and she ran back to the farm, leading the unbrushed pony, with joy rising in her like a tide.

Thus, the way of it began. Rushing through her chores to have more time at the pool, the gloss on the pony's coat shimmered more than usual as their entwined murmurings bound them together in enchantment, nurtured by the magic of the glade. She told no one of their meetings but suspected that some mornings on her return her father cast a querying eye at the pony's coat, each day now glowing brighter as did her eyes. Sometimes the two of them would go for a short stroll, but she found his long stride hard to match, even though he'd strangely shaped feet, or so it seemed from his boots, foreshortened as they were. She was shy of asking about this, however, worried that he felt ashamed of this disfigurement, cautious of embarrassing him.

He'd found six weeks work with a local blacksmith. A pair of ornate gates had been ordered for the drive leading up to one of the few big houses in the Kingdom. A major landowner wanted to show off his well doing.

As they talked, their spirits leaned more and more towards each other. Aware of the six weeks passing oh so quickly, they talked of deeper and deeper feelings and deeper and deeper yearnings, but they never touched, conscious of the heartbreak which could lie down that road. As the last meeting came ever nearer, their souls grew closer but their hearts began to sink.

The last morning dawned. She dragged her feet on the way to the pool. She did not want their last meeting to be over. Bowed and downcast when they met, he began to speak sadly but with resignation.

"So now today, I have to tell you the part of my tale I've not yet told".

She listened to the story of a breed of creatures called 'kelpies'. Shapeshifters they were, changing from man to horse. A story of him not fitting in with them, his own race. Indeed, coming to abhor their evil leanings and the wild twisted joy their natures led them to when in horse-shape. They delighted at low tide in luring riders onto their backs and then would leap into any nearby water drowning their passengers. He spoke of his need to leave the company of these creatures with whom he could no longer be comfortable. Of coming to the Kingdom, where he'd heard the people were gentle and accepting of those who were different.

She wept at his feeling of shame in being what he was, asked what could be done.

"Nothing. I can't settle anywhere, make a place for myself when at the neap tide each month, my other nature could take over and I could do harm to those around me."

But she had listened to the man for these past weeks and knew his honourable core, and she was also skilled with horses, hearing the whispers of their souls. She felt comfortable and safe with him, knew she could trust both parts of the creature before her.

She also knew herself… and knew that she deeply loved the whole of him.

Throwing herself into his arms she wove out the web of their future.

"Da'll give us some land as my dowry, and we'll set up, you in a smithy, and me breeding fine strong horses. Each neap tide, we'll stay indoors together. I'll watch over you. keep you safe. Here with me you'll settle, and we'll live out our time contented together."

And so it was.

The demand for his metalwork grew alongside the number of animals brought to his door to be shod. She bred fine good-natured beasts, as well as three much loved and loving children, who were as happy with horses as with humans. No-one questioned their routines, least of all the grandparents, when the grandchildren stayed with them for a few days every month. No-one wondered why the smithy regularly closed for just a day or two. It was generally agreed that a couple so obviously in love deserved some time alone together. And for the rest of their long and happy lives, no-one but her saw him with his boots off, and saw that instead of feet, at the end of his long long legs, he had two beautiful strong shiny hooves.

Roots

They both lived in the longest of the Kingdom's glens, Glenfad. Narrow at its top, seeming to caress the skyline, this particular glen rolled downward, its green sward swaying and curving past small hills, bouncing streams and huge ice-abandoned boulders. It was like a river flowing, or a long skirt ever widening until its hem spread out to rest on the shore.

She lived close to the glen top on her tiny farm, growing most of what she ate, collecting the herbs she needed for her poultices and ointments. Her cottage cradled her as she pounded her mortar, breathing the clean air of the high lands, smelling the aromas of the blended plants, all against a background thrum from her beloved black cat.

He lived in a different world. A fisherman, his roots were right at the shore, his cottage low as protection from the sea winds. Dark inside, it had few windows to keep out the regular sea frets, ever tugging at the walls. Those windows sometimes even turned spray when the sea horses galloped high on the waves at full tide. The smells of his home were of damp clothes drying around the peat fire, and of freshly gutted fish being smoked in the rafters.

It was the sheerest of chances that they met at all at a Hiring Fair in a neighbouring glen. She rarely left her heights, others doing any necessary buying for her, but her pestle, which had ground so much for so many, had finally become ground down itself. Only she could choose the one which fitted itself into her hand from those made by the town mason in Glen Dara. So, she accepted a lift across to the next glen in her neighbours' cart, when they were going to the May Hiring Fair there.

He rarely strayed from where he could smell sea salt but knew of a woman in Glen Dar who reared her own flock of a special breed of sheep. She spun and knit their lanolin-full coats into thick warm sweaters which were famed for being the most waterproof in the Kingdom. Though the last one he'd bought had survived the soakings of many seasons he now needed another. So, he accepted a lift to the May Hiring Fair in his neighbours' cart, they going to the fair, and he to the wife of the mason for it was she who made these singular garments.

The two arrived at the same time and drank tea while their items were chosen, and their purchasing was made. Thrust together by the hospitality of their hosts, they emerged at the same time from the mason's home. Each had agreed to wait at the same spot for their neighbours' carts for the journey home. There was a bench under an oak tree in that town to which the people of the Kingdom were often drawn without knowing why, aware only that it brought them peace.

Finding the bench empty -everyone was busy at the Fair- they sat beside each other to wait under the rustling oak leaves. Little was spoken, as if living alone for so long had left them with only so much conversation at any one time, and that had already been used up during the buying. But each recognised this in the other and were at ease in the mutual silence of the other's company. The comfort of this contact with another was strange to them both, the pull of it deep. As the waiting time passed, the bench worked its magic as it often did for those who lived in that place. They felt a warmth as strong as a hug pass from one to the other, and they relaxed in its mutual embrace. By the time their neighbours came for them, their reluctance to break this intimate connection was so strong that the thought of resuming their solitary lives pushed them to agree to another meeting in a fortnight. It would be a long walk from Glenfad to Dara Glen for them both, but their need to connect again, now woken, would not be stilled.

So, they met… and the next time only strengthened that need. Each week, right throughout that long lovely summer, their quiet natures came together and soothed and comforted and joined until they became part of the other. By the end of the autumn, they knew they wanted to live the rest of their lives at each other's side.

However, there was one main obstacle to this. Each had a cottage and a livelihood and deep roots in different parts of Glenfad. Saying that few plants grew in the winter, she tried first. Leaving her few animals with her neighbours telling them to eat the eggs and drink the milk in return for their caring, she and her cat moved down to the shore at the beginning of winter. As the months passed, the darkness of his home bowed in on her. Her eyes ran with the sting of the peat smoke and her clothes smelt of dried fish. The frequent mists blocked her sight and settled in her chest bringing a hacking cough, all of which wearied her soul.

Seeing this, he said that there was little fishing in the wintertime, and the two of them and the cat moved up to the top of the glen into her cottage. She breathed deeply of the fresh air and pulled the long views of the valley into her soul. The cough left and the spring in her step returned. He, used to a winter huddle over a peat fire, felt his body freeze in the unchecked winds of the high glen, and was uncomfortable and vulnerable being surrounded by so much space. He missed the gulls complaining, the tides' scrape on the shingle, and the feel of salt on his skin and in his mouth. They accepted that each needed to be in their homeplace during the middle of the year, she for her herbs and he for his fishing and both for nourishing their roots. But what of the winter months?

Then the miracle happened!

Visitors from outside had often tried to tell those who lived in the Kingdom of the mountains of fire and molten red rivers which had created its shape, hills and glens, and the curves and ripples of its earth. Its inhabitants would listen and nod and smile. For them, it was enough that the Kingdom existed and that they lived there. Then came the Night of the Moving Earth. The landscape shivered in the darkness. Afterwards mothers would ensure good behaviour by telling their children of stirring giants under the ground, tossing and turning in their sleep so that the land trembled. By the morning, the unsettling had died away, and afterwards was just remembered as a time of curiosity, as a dating mark of babies born or people dying before or after that particular night.

But in a town in the middle of Glenfad there was an unusual reminder.

A large sinkhole, about seven feet deep, thirty feet wide and shaped like a saucer, had appeared at the edge of the town. Looking down into the space in the morning light, the townsfolk could see the remains of a building with the lower parts of its walls still intact. The roots of a yew tree could also be seen threading through these ruins. Everyone was stupefied. After scrabbling through the archives, references were found about a dwelling in that spot many centuries before, which had suddenly disappeared overnight. An open meeting was held about the future of this phenomenon. None of the locals were keen to claim it… who would want to live in such a hollow in the ground?

But two people did, at least during every winter. They had been looking for new roots to add to their old ones and felt that the very earth of the glen which they loved, had sympathized with their plight. The Kingdom had created a solution specially for them. At the meeting they asked, if no one else wanted them, could they please have the ruins of the Root House as the place had come to be called? Paperwork was drawn up as, of course, there were no existing deeds. The property was registered in both their names, and in time re-registered after their wedding changed two surnames into one.

The townsfolk, while wary of it, were quietly proud of their new attraction, which brought the curious and thus more business to the town. Many of them, in the way of the kinship of the place, helped flatten out the site during the rest of that summer, and while still low and sheltered, it lost its underground echoes and feel. In such free time as they had, they also helped with the restoration of the building - repairing the walls, steadying the floors, putting on a roof. Most of the root was removed but the ground around the base of the yew itself was planted with ivy and wild honeysuckle, which over the coming years could use what was left as a trellising.

By the next winter, she and the cat were able to move down the glen, and he moved up. Together they rooted in their new home, the place where they could mesh together contentedly for part of each year. During the rest of each year, in their respective cottages, they would pause several times each day and look in the direction of the other's home, smiling a quiet smile. Deep in their once lonely hearts, they knew that there, in the other's homeplace as well as in the Root House, they were truly loved.

The Heir to the Estate

He lived in Glenbreen in one of the few big houses in the Kingdom. Not a particularly ornate home, in fact in many ways quite understated. There were the usual rooms of paintings and curiosities, and extensive gardens full of exotic vegetation, all brought back from the various wanderings of his ancestors. Being an only child, and unusually the son of two only children, there was, however, an absence of one thing - other people. No brothers, sisters, cousins or other family to bring the house to life, with voices, footfall, laughter and busyness. His mother had died giving birth to him. His grieving, and thus increasingly taciturn, father followed her with relief when his son was only twenty-one. The heir devoted the next few years to taking over all the financial pots his father had stirred and to consolidating the running of the estate.

He found himself at the age of thirty-one before he even realised. That was still young for a man, so now with all turning like greased clockwork, he looked around him for a wife. But this proved to be more of a challenge than he expected. He knew he was of the Kingdom, loving it with a passion as all around him did. His roots there were as sound as the oldest of its inhabitants. He breathed its soft air with gratitude that he lived there, not somewhere else.

However, at the age of seven, he'd been sent to a boarding school far to the south. On the face of it, to learn the best ways to run an estate but in reality, because his looks and ways were so like those of his mother that his father preferred to avoid a constant reminder of his lost love. When his father died before his time, the young man had cut short his education and returned home to use his education to improve the estate as best he could. That had been a time-consuming task over many busy years, so it came as a surprise to him, when seeking a spouse, to find that those who lived nearby were wary of him. Was he still one of them, or had an invisible wall been erected by his absence… and also his wealth? He wouldn't marry outside the Kingdom. Its deep river of knowledge and knowing, of belonging and being, ran deep in him, but it seemed that only he was sure of that when it came to a possible marriage.

There were only a few families in the Kingdom as well off as he. During the years he was busy taking over the estate, all the potential wealthy brides had long since been married off, with the best possible financial advantage for all concerned. Though in truth he didn't care if any future bride had money or not – he had plenty. But how would he meet those who were of the poorer families? How comfortable would they feel living his lifestyle? Anyway, they too had already had their share of arranged marriages.

Everywhere he looked he saw couples. He'd no school friends from the Kingdom, cousins or any other family to invite him to their homes. There were no family weddings or funerals to attend, the traditional meeting place of future pairings. He tried turning up at one of the local pubs one evening and chatting to the men he found there, but as many of them worked for him, his presence had led to stilted conversation and a sense of uneasy company. There was nothing he could do but continue to rattle round the Big House on his own, keeping busy with the estate and his account books. This unsatisfactory state of affairs continued for some time with his mood creeping ever closer to despair through sheer loneliness.

One day, out riding to work off some energy and ease his edginess, he came across the scene of an accident on the path ahead. One of the gypsy caravans which regularly crossed the Kingdom mending use-worn pots and age-worn tools, had overturned. The driver lay to one side, his neck at an unnatural crooked angle. The horse had somehow broken away from the shaft. Standing further down the path, sweat flecked, white eyed, it was still breathing deeply in shock, loose reins dangling from its neck. A woman lay on the ground with part of the broken shaft protruding from her torso, creating a crimson rose on her breast, her face white and still. It was obvious that nothing could be done for them. So, with gentle words and actions, he first calmed the horse, tethering it to a tree with the broken reins.

Now what? He couldn't right the wagon himself but thought that for honour's sake, he should straighten the two bodies and cover them if he could, give them back some dignity before they were seen by anyone to whom he'd go for help. Pulling back the curtain at the front of the caravan and peering into the gloom to find a covering of some sort in the overturned jumble, he found himself staring into the shocked unblinking eyes of a boy peering out from under a length of wood, possibly part of a shelf. Trying not to disturb the caravan's contents, he reached out in the direction of the eyes and found himself holding a small hand. Carefully lifting away the wood, he eased the tiny figure out into the open air. The boy slumped down at the side of the track, on the other side of the wreckage away from the bodies.

Not knowing what else to do, the rider simply sat beside him, wrapping him in his arms. He held him until he felt awareness replacing shock, life slowly creeping back into the small form.

"Where are Ma and Da? Are my brother and sister still in there?" whispered a shaky voice.

After as quick a search as possible among the precarious contents of the broken caravan, two other tiny rag-doll bodies were brought out onto the grass beside their brother. They made a pitiful trio. Two boys possibly seven and five, and a girl of about two, all small of frame, with brown faces ringed by dark curls, and the biggest staring eyes he'd yet seen in any human face. They sat silent, unmoving. Even their breasts scarcely rose or fell with their breathing.

"Ma and Da?" came the query again.

His answer produced no reaction. The children watched without emotion as he covered their parents' bodies with a tarpaulin. Their shock was a merciful anaesthetic.

What else was to be done now but to take them back to the Big House? Fashioning a sling from his horse blanket across his chest, he placed the inert girl inside it, across his heart hoping that the strong beat of his pulse would somehow sustain her. He walked the horse home, balancing the two boys on its back. Handing them all over to the housekeeper to be warmed, fed, washed and re-clothed, he next contacted the local undertaker. A group was sent from the Home Farm to clear the wreckage and bring the horse and anything else which could be salvaged back to the House.

In the next few weeks - when it felt as if time stood still for all - while arranging the funeral, he tried to find out about the children to see what to do with them next. They knew so little! In their short wandering lives in the caravan, friendships had been brief and passing. Some relatives were mentioned but there was no knowledge of their whereabouts. Their parents had been the only steady feature of their young lives. At least they knew their parents' names to go on the headstone but little else. They themselves, Jem (James), Joe (Joseph) and Lucy, were all they could name of their particular branch of the O'Brian family.

As days passed, and they increasingly reverted to being children rather than survivors, he found that for him they had begun to fill part of the emptiness in his life. As a result, when the Vicar and the Governor of the small local orphanage arrived at the door together one day to discuss the children's future, he realised that he had already decided where it would be - at the Big House with him. They had been left with nobody. He had been left with nobody. Now in future the four of them would have each other. He would officially take them on as Wards. So, what if some people thought he was mad, muttering about his insanity at taking three gypsies into the house! Many more spoke of his charity and big-heartedness. No-one knew that he felt he'd been given a miraculous gift.

The love of the four for each other grew as the little ones grew in stature. The children grew in knowledge as well when he hired a local young widow to become their governess. His life then became complete when he and the governess developed feelings for each other. The children were the ringbearers at their wedding. But never a day passed when, in gratitude for his family, he did not often thank Mr and Mrs O'Brian who had made it all possible. He hoped they blessed him as much as he blessed them.

The Gift from the Sea

One part of the Kingdom sat apart from the rest. t the end of a finger of land stretched out into the sea, eleven cottages clustered together. They held thirty to forty people, from grandparents to children, most of them from seven different families. At the point where this spur connected with the rest of the Kingdom, the land lay low on the ground, often covered by the tide, seldom free from overnight mists which in winter became semi-permanent. It was easier to reach the houses at the spur's tip by boat than to walk the causeway.

The people there lived close, dependent on each other for food, working together on each other's fields. They hunted rabbits, fished, collected shellfish from the beach and birds' eggs from the cliffs along the shore. A few would go to the nearest market once a fortnight for any supplies needed from outside their tiny settlement. They were small and wiry on their diet, but content in their daily lives, secure in the knowledge that the other cottagers were circling and supporting their minds and their hearts.

When the young grew to an age when they got restless, often they would leave and then return after a while, tired of the world's busy ways and its noise. They wanted back to the soothing routine of living with the seasons, the peace of the shore's edge and the sound of the wind and gulls heard in the wide sky. Sometimes they brought back a spouse, some of whom folded into the place with ease. Others stayed as long as they could stand it and then left, back to their previous world, leaving new babes and young toddlers who then melded with those among whom they had been born.

If any of the turfed roofs of the cottages heard complaints or sharp remarks around the fire, it was kept up among the eaves. Sharp tongues soon found themselves with no-one to listen. If any complaint had a solid ring to it, it was sorted by all at a general meeting in the small church. This was the only communal building, though it was well understood that the priest's voice only had the same weight as all the others. Everyone contributed to their survival, so each had their own equal say. A rich life… or a poor one, depending on whether you valued people or possessions. For those at the spar's end, the days rolled past, year by year, with little change.

Until the year of the Great Storm. The cottagers were well used to storms, usually nestling in their homes until they passed, afterwards rejoicing in the driftwood swept up onto the beach. But this time it was different! It was a summer storm, baked in heat, with loud rolls of thunder and bright forks of lightning, followed by heavy fat raindrops welcomed by all as they broke the dark heaviness of the air and cleared their heads. When it had passed, and they poured out of their homes to breathe in great lungfuls of fresh air, they found a gift left by the waves.

A small rowing boat had been sea-cast onto the beach, with broken timbers and a gaping hole in the keel. In its bottom, a young figure lay, unconscious, salt-rimed, water-beaten. With care, some of them lifted out the girl - for it was a she - and laid her flat on the sand, finding to their relief that she still lived. Dark of skin and hair, slender of form and delicate of feature, had she had a tail, the children would have thought her a mermaid. But no, she was just a girl, though an exotic one. She was taken to the parochial house where the priest's housekeeper could nurse her back to consciousness. Then they'd find out how she came to be there, stranded alone in a boat on their beach.

But the answer didn't come soon, as she lay for more than two nights without moving. The housekeeper slow-dripped first water and then weak broth into her, so that she wouldn't choke. When she did stir and her eyes opened, she jerked into life with fear, pulling back into a ball of taut limbs in a corner of the pallet bed, huge eyes staring. Her dread eased when she saw the kindness in their eyes. Her body released its tightened curl. However, the first sounds from her strained throat were not the tongue they knew, but a different language altogether from a foreign land.

Over the next few days, as the housekeeper nourished the girl but starved the neighbours of news, shooing them all away from the door to give her peace to rest, the priest made some headway in communicating. He'd worked out she was Italian. With gestures, rough drawings and some Latin from his clerical training, basic facts emerged. Leaving Italy and sailing north-west, she and her father were going to build a new life for themselves after her mother's death. An apothecary, her father had died onboard of a fever. The ship's captain, seeing her defenceless, had made his intentions clear – he would keep her on board as his slave. And then the storm broke. Seeing an opportunity while his attention was fully occupied elsewhere, she had untied a small lifeboat and threw both it and herself overboard. Better to risk a death at sea than the life the Captain intended for her! Managing to pull herself into it, she prepared to die as the tiny wooden shell was thrown from wave crest to wave crest. Passing out in terror, her next memory was the faces of those on the beach, showing caring concern and worry.

As she grew stronger and conversation became easier between them, the priest suggested that she go to the main harbour in the Kingdom to continue her journey, but she recoiled from that. Could she not stay here in the Kingdom, in this cluster of cottages where she felt safe? She had never been to the lands in the north-west, had neither papers nor money, nothing to go back to in Italy. She'd lived off poor land growing up and had learnt many of her father's skills. Could she not try that here? The more the priest tried to dissuade her, the more resolute she became. After a while he appeared to surrender, thinking that one winter's practical reality would change her mind where reason would not.

At a general meeting to discuss the situation, it soon became very clear however, that the cottagers saw the girl as a gift to them from the sea, felt responsible for her in some atavistic pagan way which the priest's religion did not explain. A small one-roomed dwelling had been abandoned when the last dissatisfied wife had left the village. Her husband and children had moved back in with his parents who needed his strong back and the children's nimble fingers. It was decided. The cottagers would repair the dwelling, each as they could, furnish it enough so she could sleep, cook, and keep a fire. They'd show her how to catch the fish, climb the cliffs for eggs, hunt the wild rabbits - whatever it took to keep their lucky giftling with them. The rest of what she needed she'd get by using the skill of healing she'd inherited from her father. The sea had given her to them from one life, they declared. They'd not throw her back with ingratitude to another, and they proved to be just as determined as she. So the priest kept his counsel and let them get on with their plan, for truly he too had fallen under the same spell which had enchanted them, respecting her gentle ways, the grace in her first faltering steps and the shining purity of her soul.

Time passed. It was as if the very land itself welcomed her. When the dwelling was complete, they used the rocks left on the beach by the sea tides to create two walled fields, one for potatoes and vegetables and the other for the herbs and flowers needed for her cures. Each house gave a few seedlings to her to get her started. The earth rewarded her with an abundance of all that she touched, so that she was able to repay everyone by the end of the next season. Birds began to nest on the cliffs in such numbers that their eggs became plentiful. Rabbits grew so many that stews never seemed to be without the taste of meat. Shoals of such size, not seen for many generations, stayed for months along the shoreline, providing fresh fish in the summer, with many more dried in barrels for the winter months.

She proved to be as capable of dealing with animals as with people. Flocks of sheep and clutches of hens thrived and provided. But it was the people who, to outside eyes, changed most. The children grew tall and strong, the mothers gave birth to full-term lusty babes, the men now lived long and hearty lives. Before, life on this bleak spar of land had been so hard that its people thinned and failed, coughing and wheezing to an early grave.

What of her, the gift from the sea? Although her dark colouring, soft ways and the slight accent she'd never lost when using their tongue, enticed many suitors, both among the cottagers and from farther afield, her experience with the sea captain had been enough for her of the ways of men. She never married. She didn't lack for children or family though for didn't all who lived in the cottages love and honour her. Most of her food, clothes and belongings were gifts, the giving of which was never spoken about, but now few who lived at the spar's end ailed or sickened. Furthermore, the natural accidents which happened to all those who live on the land, healed fast with little pain and few lasting scars, thanks to her care.

'Regalo dal mare' she laughingly called herself, 'the gift from the sea' in Italian. 'Mare' was close enough to the common Kingdom name Maire for it to become more widely used than her own unfamiliar Italian one.

Maire was the name eventually etched on her tombstone in the small graveyard beside the church. She was laid to rest in a sheltered corner, surrounded by a happy lifesworth of people who had loved her. There the sound of the waves on the seashore from whence she'd come, could always be heard.

Without Words

He tidied the two rooms in the tiny cottage in Glenorlar yet again. Well, 'tidied' was too grand a word for what he did. The rooms had little furniture and he'd already tidied that morning, so there was really nothing to do. He brushed the clean floor, straightened the already aligned delph on the dresser, checked there was enough kindling and logs indoors for when he'd light the fire that evening. Then he went back outside, sitting down on the chair just outside the doorway, with its long rolling view down the glen to the shore.

On that late autumn afternoon, the horizon showed the evening sea mist already starting to roll in. The trees and bushes nearby rippled with the movements of birds and insects, fussing in their bedding down for the night, searching for the last of the day's food, making sure their roosts or refuges were as clean, dry and comfortable as they could make them. He scanned the view below him but nothing important had changed. It never did.

His wife had died eight years ago, the children had been gone for over thirty, and his neighbours had left the cottage at the other end of the lane five years since. Still a spritely man in himself at seventy-two, his children, having done well, sent a monthly sum so that he didn't want for anything.

"You don't have to farm any more, Da."

This monthly gift eased their consciences. Paying it freed them from having to make the long journey up the glen to see him more than once every couple of months. It was their way of sliding out of obligation and into the freedom of neglecting him. For him it meant a slow descent into lethargy and loneliness.

He could have moved closer to the shore, but this was his place both man and boy. Born in the settle beside the fire, he'd grown here, inherited the place from his father, brought his bride home to it in the heady triumphant flush of winning her. Together they'd raised their family within these four sturdy walls, celebrating many milestone happenings. Now he was alone except for the ghosts of familiar lively faces and the echoes of joyous contented laughter in every nook and cranny and round every turn. How could he leave a place which was the sum of his life's living? So, he stayed, fading a little more each day.

Until the day when the loaded cart had clattered past his door, rolling to a halt in front of the run-down empty cabin at the other end of the lane. Not wanting to intrude, at first, he stayed indoors but after a while took his usual seat outside the front door. He could only see the outline of the gable end of the other cottage through the thinning autumnal branches of the trees, but he could hear childish voices, high with the novelty of the day, the cottage, the place. A thin stream of smoke began to snake upwards from one of its two chimneys.

When an emptied cart trolled past his door again heading down the glen, he was torn between a reticence to stay in his own safe space and an instinct towards neighbourliness. Coming to a decision, he smoothed his hair with well water and packed an offering of firewood and some cheese and potatoes into a hessian bag. Straightening his shoulders, he stepped along the lane to see if he could help the newcomers.

It was not what he'd expected, though in truth, he hadn't had any real preconceptions. Outside the cottage the space was already clean and clear, with the contents of the cart already ensconced inside its four walls.

"They mustn't have had much," was his immediate thought.

The sound of young voices burbled through the open door. In response to a loud deliberate cough, two bundles of life tumbled out, sparking with excitement, eager to greet a newcomer. Words poured out of them. With little prompting from him, he soon learned their whole tale to date. They were brother and sister, she eleven and protective of her eight-year-old sibling who resented her three years' dominance. Their widowed mother had died last month of a consumption. The landlord had served an eviction notice within a week of the funeral; he'd had a better paying tenant already lined up. Granny, who'd lived with them since Granda died long before their birth, was some distant kin of the cottage owners. They'd offered it Granny to rent at a minimal cost. After all, they were family, and she now needed a roof under which to rear the two young ones.

The information continued to flow. Moving here from a farm down at the Glen's foot, they knew the ways of growing and rearing. They were truly well off, having a sow, a goat and five chickens plus tools and seeds for planting next Spring, all given to them by caring folk after their mother passed. Oh, and there'd be more coming in, as their granny was known far and wide as a clever seamstress, as good at creating the new as mending the worn. And they'd be able to repair any neglect to the cottage themselves as they were both strong and hard working.

Had they mentioned their Granny was deaf since birth and had never learned to speak? It was grand though as the family had worked out their own way of signing, so they chatted together all the time… just in a different way to other people. Eventually, having poured all this over him and wound down a little, the girl went inside to tell of their visitor.

Hand pulled by her grand-daughter; Granny was almost dragged out the cottage door to meet him. She was a tall soft-faced woman in her mid-fifties, greying of hair, straight of shoulder and piercing of gaze as if her eyes took in what her ears could not. In that first out-stretching of hands to shake, and in the first long look they exchanged, almost as much knowledge passed between them as he had learned from the children. She saw the impact of his living alone in his hesitancy to touch her hand and his lack of surety in approaching her, but she also saw his trustworthiness in the way the children were already looking up at him without reserve. She saw the laughter lines at his eyes and mouth, and his thoughtful kindness in the contents of the bag he proffered as a welcome gift. He saw her determination to make the cottage not only habitable but a home, despite the reserve her deafness had forced on her, separating her from others as it did. He also sensed her awareness and anxiety that the way forward would be hard for her, a woman alone, in nurturing two young children safely to adulthood.

That first long look forged a bond. In the knowing way of the Kingdom, the two were already aware that in the coming years, neither would ever be alone again, drawn together as they would be by their own needs as well as those of the children. They were right. Over the years ahead, both cottages did indeed become filled with life, laughter, love and togetherness once more.

The Tide of Life

The boy, stretching out his legs, slid back into a comfortable position against the tree trunk. Turning his closed eyes up to the warm May sun he let his mind drift. He was long-legged like a young colt, nut brown in hue with tousled hair. Lean but not skinny, fine-boned but strong-sinewed, he had seen fourteen May Days come and go. For the first ten he'd been living with his Da, a fisherman in a one-roomed cottage at the shore of Glenfad, his mother losing her life while giving her firstborn his. He and his Da had rarely spoke but lived together in close harmony. Each knew their tasks - when and where they had to be, what each had to do to ensure that the circle of their lives continued to turn smoothly. Although at the time of the Great Storm, his Da had turned his small boat shoreward in cautious time, the wind had had its own plan. The boat was last seen heading towards the edge of the light, disappearing forever into the sea mists.

Those of the Kingdom would never see an orphan lost for shelter. At first, he'd been taken in by a retired shop owner and his new wife, but their life of gentle words, relaxed days, and especially their desire to send him to the local school, did not sit well with him. He was a restless and independent youngling, whose nature had been forged by a life of tides and currents, sun and storms, striving days and silent evenings. So, they came to an understanding, realising he could not be tamed and caged, but needed care all the same. Food, and occasionally clothing, was left in their lean-to. From time-to-time, fish, some wild earthy mushrooms or handfuls of wild garlic would be found there in return.

The boy never realised that his Da's hut, where he now sheltered, was regularly visited when he was out, to check that pots and pans, bedding and knives, and the other items necessary for even the most basic living, were always there and usable. He never questioned when he found replacements for the things he needed, abandoned within a reasonable radius of his lair. Despite his father's death, he trusted, in the way of the Kingdom, that what was needed would be provided, that the Fates in that place were kindly, not harsh or punishing.

As the May sun slid him into a dreamless doze, he almost missed the passing of the gypsy caravan, and was brought back to consciousness only by the snuffling of the horses and the jingle of the bells around the caravan door. Rising to his feet, in a brief exchange he directed them to the nearest suitable spot for the night. On a whim, he led them there. Ever curious, he was intrigued by how different they were. He wanted to know more. He brought them to a grassy sheltered spot which soon echoed with the noise of the horses pulling at the sweet Spring grass. A cascading stream tumbling behind them, while the domestic sounds of a fire crackled and food was prepared, he asked question after question, drinking in the answers.

There were four in the group – a father, mother and two daughters. The elder daughter was his age, busy helping her mother but glancing at him sideways when she thought no-one was looking. Then there was the younger one, the darling baby, now five, a late miracle, who made up for the two stillborn babes who'd gone before her. "My princess" the father called her, and with her sweet shy smile and dancing curls, she was indeed a princess in the making. A tightknit group in the way of their tribe, they were as intrigued by him as much as he was by them.

Surviving on his own, almost totally self-sufficient, he was skilled in the ways of nature's bounty in providing food. All of that they honoured, but they wondered, on hearing the boy's tale, why he had not chosen the easier path of staying with the retired couple. His aversion to being rooted with them, of being trapped under their roof was understood by his audience. He spoke of how he preferred the freedom to choose, when the fancy took him, to sleep under the stars, or explore the glen, or even dance on the shore. His deep desire was to make each day different, begin a fresh page each dawn he opened his eyes. The goodness of the couple humbled him but he did not want schooling or regular mealtimes or the small space of a bedroom when he could have the large awning of an open sky.

The more they talked, the more he saw how their lifeways fitted his dreams, their freedom suited his soul. They saw how his knowledge and skills could add to their family, and how the tug of their travelling lit up his eyes. Yet again by chance in the Kingdom, one of its inhabitants had stumbled across something unexpected, which provided a pathway forward and an opportunity to fulfil individual dreams. The next day, after a visit to the couple and then to his father's cottage to close those two chapters of his life, he left the Glen to begin another one. As the wagon swayed beneath him, he mused how familiar the movement was to the one he had been reared with, of his father's boat cresting the waves, riding onward towards the horizon.

Sheltered Lives

The cottage, as many were, was built for shelter in a fold of the land on the side of a glen in the heart of the Kingdom. The hill swell behind it protected it from wind. The trees on either side of it, planted in a time forgotten, with their gently whispering branches, leaned in to keep its walls safe. The grassy swathe in front of it was a blanket and a playground for babes, both animal and human.

Not a grand dwelling, it was a sturdy home, with symmetrical windows on either side of a central door, and a boarded roof space for storage, where children could also sleep. As the threshold was a huge slab of white rock hauled from the shore many years past, to some the frontage had the appearance of being friendly, even of smiling. The windows seemed like crinkling eyes, the door a straight nose and the threshold a white slash of a toothy grin, all under an overhung roughly trimmed fringe of thatch. It smiled on many, that cottage.

Two of its earliest inhabitants, according to local lore, had been a brother and sister, from a branch of the O'Leary family neither of whom had ever married. They'd both been born in the cottage and, many contented years later, died there within a few months of each other. It was he, James O'Leary, who was credited with boarding over the loft, though in truth that could have been done long before his time. His sister Jane had been famed for her baking. Few who visited ever left without a clutch of the sweetest tasting bread and buns that those in that glen of the Kingdom would ever taste.

With no children, perhaps focusing on other things yielded different results. Her carefully tended plot produced the largest vegetables ever brought to the local market. His animals were of such gentle natures and fine good health they were always in demand among his neighbours for breeding. The cottage smiled widely at them and in turn the generosity of their welcome touched each passer-by, leaving them warmed and nourished.

The next family to rent the place were glad of that welcome and warmth. They were glad too to inherit the carefully nourished abundance of the place. They'd married young and had five hale and healthy children by the time the mother reached thirty. Thus, they needed surety about the feeding and raising of them. Jane's plot continued to richly provide, and their own animals thrived and produced. Perhaps not as well as for the elderly couple, but it was certainly enough for the two of them and their younglings. After their chores, they would tumble, run, wrestle and laugh in and around their home with all the careless freedom of the well-fed and safe.

They grew and blossomed until the day when each left for work or to marry, to follow their own life path. The cottage beamed when they returned to visit with a clutch of babes and toddlers. In time the aged grandparents were laid to rest beside each other in the local graveyard, content with their life achievement, another sturdy branch added to their family tree.

The cottage next sheltered another brother and sister, but these two had moved up from the shore. They'd been raised there by their parents, their father a fisherman. They'd had a grand life, been a close family until the night of the Great Storm, when their father had gone outside in the teeth of it to check yet again that his boat was safely harnessed to the harbour wall. A rogue wave had enveloped him. Over the next ten long days before the sea surrendered his body back to the land, their mother paced up and down the shore, her eyes straining out to sea, not speaking but staring silently. The wait broke her.

After their father's burial, the brother and sister soon laid her beside him. Then they both turned their backs to the shoreline and moved inland. They were determined to live somewhere without the sound of waves pulling at shingle or gulls screaming at the horizon. They wanted quiet and security. That's what they found in the cottage on the side of the glen. The trees bent protectively over them, whispering gentle murmurings. The stone walls blocked out all memories of strong winds. The cottage coddled them through their grief, and throughout their middle and later years. They rarely left it, relishing the peace and serenity they found there. It was as if they'd used up all their ration of life's hardship. Now with it behind them, they were entitled to calm and contentment for the rest of their days.

The power of the cottage's smile was much needed by its next inhabitant. When the brother and sister finally passed after two long and gentle lives, their nest was rented out to a man who also needed nourishment and contenting, but who, in his pain, would accept none of it. From a well-respected wealthy family in the next glen, he'd married for deep love, and lost his desire for life when his wife and child both died in the process of birthing.

Sunk in his grief and most times in the bottom of a bottle, he lived on a weekly gifting from his family, who had so cut him adrift they were willing to pay the rent as well as the gifting, as long as it was for a cottage in the next glen. Living there no stain from his life could tint theirs. He ate less than he drank, railed at his misfortune more than he slept, and was tortured each day.

It was as if the cottage mourned with him. It became unkempt and untidy, walls stained with damp as if it too cried salted tears. The thatch turned thin and leaking. The wind in the trees howled louder than the sounds of the branches' comforting whispers. His anger and grief and pain kept him alive, much longer than love and comfort would have. At last, having rejected of the healing power of the place, the hollow shell of his body was found out on the road one early morning, still and silent. At last, he was at peace. And once again, so was his dwelling.

To the passing eye, the cottage now seemed a place past giving. No-one wanted to live somewhere so derelict and full of echoes from its recent past. The thatch and loft fell in, the walls crumbled. The skeleton of its building, the very stones of its walls, became increasingly visible while tree branches stretched and over-shaded the room inside. But the cottage had held onto its strong warm depths. The walls had crumbled but what was left rounded over with a soft layer of lichen. The green of the outside swathe had widened, rolled through the front door and laid a carpet of sweet soft moss over the brown earthen floor. Clumps of swaying ferns, sinuous ivy and tall majestic foxgloves became the room's new furnishings. The tree branches gave shelter in the corners from the sun's heat in summer and the weather's blast in winter.

The cottage became home to many other families over the coming years. Fox and badger cubs, baby hedgehogs and squirrel kittens all passed through, growing strong in safety before leaving to explore the Kingdom in their own ways. In the tree branches nests of wood warblers, starlings, choughs and chaffinches were rebuilt year after year to house open mouthed chicks. As these grew, they learned to swoop and glide around the walls and along the curve of the glen side. Smaller tracks of shrews and baby mice patterned the grass beside the silvered trails of snails. Intricate festoons of cobwebs laced the ruined ramparts, covering them with spider shawls. The threshold once more released its grin, the nourishing power of the place hummed, and the ruins smiled again over its own small domain within the Kingdom.

Epilogue

And so, Readers, you've now visited the Kingdom and read some of its tales.

Have you heard them before, known them all along?

Your ancestors may be calling to you.

Listen well, do you hear echoes, feel the warmth of kinship?

Perhaps your Kingdom's just out there,

waiting for you to find it…

if you remember where to look.

Appendix -

The Geography of the Kingdom

**The names of these Glens are entirely fictitious*

Glenard	(The High Glen)
Glenfad	(The Long Glen)
Dara Glen	(The Glen of the Oak Trees)
Glenbreen	(The Glen of the Fairy Dwelling)
Glendora	(The Sanctified Glen)
Leanan Glen	(Lovers Glen)
Glenorlar	(The Glen of the Eagles)

How to use the QR Codes

Open the camera app on your smart phone, then hold the camera over the QR code on the page.

Once the camera has read the QR code, it will open a web link, just like below. Click on that link to be taken to YouTube to listen to the recording of the story.

Grateful thanks to Brendan Mullen for his time, expertise and patience in recording these tales. The stories are now presented with much more clarity as a result of Brendan's talent and dedication.

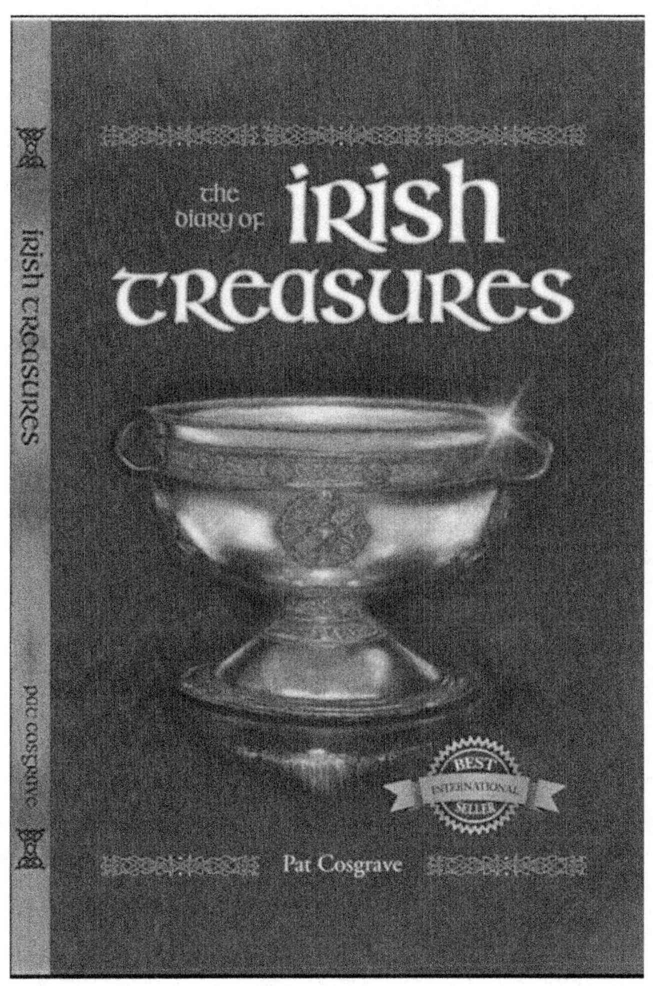
the diary of
irish
treasures
BEST
INTERNATIONAL
SELLER
Pat Cosgrave
irish treasures
pat cosgrave

About the Artist
Pat Cosgrave Biography

Pat Cosgrave studied fine art at The Vicky Harvey School of Fine Art, Brisbane, Australia. She has written and illustrated *'The Diary of Irish Treasures'* available on Amazon and now an International Bestseller.

The book is an eternal diary/journal with detailed paintings of ancient Irish artefacts – never before painted. Each painting is accompanied by a story of its find, history and current location in Ireland.
In 1989 Harper Collins published her *'Brisbane Yearbook'* featuring 52 watercolour paintings of heritage Brisbane buildings.

She specialises in children's portraits and is now experimenting with abstract work.

You can view her work on Instagram – patcosgrave7.
She was born in Belfast and is one of 10 children. She divides her time between Australia and Ireland.

About the Author

On returning from S.W. France to live in Northern Ireland, retired teacher of twenty-six years Mary Farrell joined her first Creative Writing Group in 2017. For the last four years a Facilitator of the *North Coast Writers* Group, she is now in her second year as a Judge for the Weekly Competition run by Reedsy Online Publishing Company. On behalf of Causeway u3a Creative Writing Groups, she is an auditor of selected Creative Writing classes at Ulster University in Northern Ireland. For Libraries NI, she facilitates *Words Inc,* a Coleraine Library Creative Writing Group. Mary is also a member of CIEP, the Chartered Institute of Editing and Proofreading, UK.

Her first Collection of varied pieces, *It's like Walking a Tightrope* was published in September 2021, and her second *Out of the Chrysalis* in May 2022. *Springboards: a Creative Writing Manual for Beginners through to Facilitators* was published in November 2022, all three books by Impspired Press.

Mary is the Editor of *Irish Hares and Seahorses,* Impspired Press, 2022, the first of the annual Anthologies to come from *North Coast Writers.* She read her own work on BBC Radio Ulster in September 2018, performed on stage at Tenx9 events in 2018, 2019 and 2022, and also in 2019 at Open Mic Sessions in Portstewart, Northern Ireland. Her short story, *A Tale of a Barn* won the Lurig Drama Club Competition in 2020. Recorded by the actor Ciaran Hinds on November 26th, 2020, it can be found at www.thenineglens.com. She has had various pieces of Prose and Poetry published in Magazines and Anthologies, both locally and internationally.

Printed in Great Britain
by Amazon

10861161R00068